A Caster & Fleet Christmas M...

Case of the Peculiar Pantomime

Paula Harmon
Liz Hedgecock

ISBN-13: 979-8579993816

For actors, musicians and live performers in 2020.
Here's to a brighter 2021.

1
Katherine

'We might as well shut the office for Christmas,' said Connie. 'We've closed all our cases, and no one's likely to want a detective now. What do you think?'

Reg nodded. 'We haven't had an enquiry for days.'

'You're right,' I answered, putting everything on my desk away before Connie could change her mind. 'Let's go to the tearoom and eat dainty cakes like ladies – and a gentleman – of leisure.'

'That would be lovely,' said Connie, but a shadow crossed her face. 'Although I still have gifts to buy.'

'Me too. Let's have tea, then we can go shopping together.' I glanced out of the window as I pinned my hat in place. The clouds had finally dispersed, and the London sky was a lovely dusky blue. Despite the smoke of a million chimneys, stars somehow managed to sparkle, and moonlight glimmered on the wet roofs. In the streets below, store windows were bright with displays in red and gold, and excited shoppers laden with packages full of secrets would be dodging puddles. London at Christmas was enchanting, and I couldn't wait to leave the office and soak it up.

'I don't suppose I could take the tree home?' said Reg wistfully. 'I don't like to think of it dying.' The potted fir I'd bought to make the office festive was draped with tinsel, and a tiny angel fashioned from typing paper sat on the top. Reg had tended it like his own flesh and blood, which was just as well. Every plant I touched withered in days.

'Of course,' said Connie. 'Though I don't know where we'll put it in the tearoom.'

'I'm gonna take it straight home.' Reg's face was full of delight as he folded the angel and put it carefully in his wallet. 'Can't wait till Lily sees this. It'll make her day. No one in our street has ever had a tree before Christmas Eve.'

Beaming with delight, he turned to us. 'Did you say you still had presents to buy? You two have been married to Mr L and Mr K for ever, yet all I've heard is you complaining about what to get them. Rose's gift was easy.' An expression reminiscent of a rabbit halfway through a particularly succulent lettuce leaf settled on his face. Albert still looked at Connie like that sometimes, though James and I were far less sentimental. Reg hefted the tree and bounded out of the office with the same energy he'd had when we first met him, whistling a love song.

Connie sighed. 'I may have been married to Albert for ever, but buying presents seems to get harder every year. Did you get James that meerschaum pipe he wanted?'

I pulled a face. 'No, I didn't. He has a perfectly good

briar one and the design he fancies is so old-fashioned it reminds me of my grandfather. I've bought him an up-to-the-minute Waterman fountain pen instead. Father and Thirza are easy, but I've no idea what to buy Margaret. She can't possibly need another handbag.'

'Ed?'

'I wanted to buy him a horse on wheels but James says that's too dull. He wants to get Ed a drum and building blocks, and he's probably right. Children that age just want noisy toys, or things to throw so that they can break something. For example, Mother's spirit.'

Connie chuckled. 'How true. When are you travelling to your in-laws?'

'Christmas Eve. Don't worry, we'll be at your party the night before, although I shall be as wide as I'm tall by New Year with all the feasting.'

'That'll be the day,' said Connie, buttoning her coat. 'We could feed you plum pudding for a fortnight and you'd still be thin as a willow.' She gave my hand a squeeze. 'It's been a good year for Caster and Fleet though, hasn't it?'

'Very,' I agreed. 'Plenty of interesting cases, and not so much danger that the men made a fuss.'

'You mean not so much danger that we had to tell them about it.' We grinned at each other. 'At least now I can sort out Christmas without a case hanging over me.'

'Do you mean presents? I suppose your family is enormous.'

Connie raised her eyebrows. 'Cheek.'

'I meant your sisters and their children, not just yours. Come on; tea and cake await, then we'll go gift-hunting.

All the shops are open late and we can get ideas from the displays in Oxford Street.' I especially hoped for an idea about a present for Connie. What do you get someone who can afford anything?

'It's not just the gifts, it's the food,' said Connie, checking that the cupboard was locked. 'I half-wish I was a child again, when all I had to do was hope I'd get the toy I wanted and a dress that made me feel like a princess. It's lovely having the children, of course, but I do miss being free to say to you, "Bother the men, let's go to the music hall—"'

The outer door of the building banged open downstairs, bringing a draught and the distant squawk of carol singers. Footsteps clattered upwards.

Connie pointed at the ceiling. 'That's bound to be for Harker and Co.' But even as she said it the footsteps slowed, and we both knew the client was not for Mr Harker.

A sharp rap rattled our door. I opened it, half-hoping there was some mistake, but at the same time feeling a familiar flicker of excitement. In the shadows of the landing stood a woman with a heavily frilled cape and a flamboyant hat.

'Selina!' I exclaimed as she stepped into the light, revealing a familiar, freckled face. 'We were just talking about the music hall.'

'How do,' she said. As she entered the office she smiled at us, but her eyes were worried.

'We're going to the tearoom,' said Connie. 'Do join us.'

'It might be better to go to the Dog and Duck,' said

Selina. 'When you hear what I've got for you, you may want something stronger than tea.'

'A pot of Assam tea, please.' I glanced at Selina. 'Would you like anything?'

'A Chelsea bun, please,' said Selina, 'if that's all right.'

'What a good idea,' said Katherine.

'And three Chelsea buns, please,' I added.

'Very good, madam,' said the waitress, and whisked away.

The teashop was busy. All around us were women: some with excited faces, some who appeared fatigued. Most had brown-paper parcels with them, either displayed on the table, or tucked discreetly beneath. I wondered where the men were, and suspected they were either still at work, or possibly in the Dog and Duck.

'So…?' Katherine enquired of Selina.

Selina twisted in her seat, looking first to the left, then the right. I would have thought such a proceeding would attract attention, but she seemed reasonably satisfied with the outcome. She leaned forward and murmured under her breath, *'There's something going on.'*

Katherine smiled. 'There's always something going on at the Merrymakers. What sort of something?'

'That's the thing,' said Selina. 'I dunno.'

Her pregnant pause was interrupted by the noisy setting-down of a tray with tea things and a plate of large indigestible-looking buns. 'Ooooh, lovely,' she said. 'Shall I be mother?'

'Why not,' I said, and watched her pour the tea. Selina looked her old healthy self once more, after a narrow escape some time before, but I noted that she gripped the teapot very firmly. I separated the buns onto different plates, and waited for Selina to begin.

'You're gonna think I've lost my marbles,' she blurted out. 'Or that I'm spinning a yarn. I'm not, honest.' She sipped her tea. 'I've never believed in mumbo-jumbo and things going bump in the night, you know that. But I've never seen – no, not seen. I've never *felt* like this.'

Katherine broke a piece off her bun and popped it into her mouth. 'Felt like what, Selina?'

Selina sighed. 'I'll start from the beginning, shall I?'

I gave her a reassuring smile. 'That would be an excellent idea.'

Selina took a large bite of her bun and chewed it, perhaps to give her strength for the coming ordeal. 'It all began with the rehearsals for the Christmas pantomime,' she said. 'Mr T is anxious to get it spot on, as it's always a money-maker. Cinderella this year, and I'm Buttons. Ellen is Cinders, of course, and Mr T and Dan Datchett are the Ugly Sisters. We've got an up-and-coming actress to play

Prince Charming, and I have to say that Mr T has done us proud with this year's props.' She took another bite of her bun, and Katherine and I waited patiently.

'So we were excited, naturally, and feeling quite festive, and the rehearsals were going well. Except my Buttons costume was never where I'd hung it when I went to get it the next day, and nor was Ellen's. I thought maybe Edie, the seamstress, had moved them, but Edie swore blind she hadn't touched a thing. Then on Wednesday afternoon the rouge disappeared; not a pot to be found anywhere. I knocked on the men's door and told them to give it back, but theirs had gone too. And by the time we had to get ready for that evening's show, it had been put back.'

'How odd,' said Katherine, frowning.

'Isn't it,' said Selina. 'It felt like someone was trying to stop us from rehearsing. Then the noises started. Never while we were performing our usual show, you understand. Only when we was rehearsing Cinderella.'

'What sort of noises?' I asked.

'Weird noises,' said Selina firmly. 'Ellen was doing the song where she sits by the hearth wishing she could go to the ball, and all of a sudden her voice tailed off and she sort of stiffened. When the band stopped, we heard a moaning noise from the wings. Dan Datchett went and had a look, but he saw nothing and joked that it was probably the wind coming in. We all laughed and felt much better, and thought no more of it.'

I smiled. 'So there was a logical explanation.'

Selina took a long draught of her tea. 'Yes,' she said. 'For that. And then we started performing it. Six days a week, two shows on Saturdays, and every other day or so, something goes wrong. When we turned up on Tuesday to get ready, the men's costumes were in our dressing room, and vice versa. And yesterday I was going on stage when out of the corner of my eye I saw a peculiar figure hurry away, as if he didn't want to be seen.'

I frowned. 'A peculiar figure?'

Selina managed a wan smile. 'I know we're all dressed up, but this person was in a long dark robe. Like a monk. I couldn't follow him, of course; I had to go on and say my lines. But when I got off stage I asked everybody, and no one else had seen him.' She gave us a triumphant look. 'What do you think of that?'

'It's certainly intriguing,' said Katherine. 'What do you want us to do?'

Selina raised her eyebrows. 'Why, investigate, of course.'

'Oh,' I said. 'We've just closed the office for Christmas.'

Selina's eyes narrowed. 'I was hoping you could help a friend,' she said. 'Seeing as you've earned quite a bit of money from us over the years. Both in your professional capacity, and on the side.' She swallowed her last piece of bun. 'I have to go: duty calls. But I hope you'll take it on. I don't mind telling you that it's rattled me, and poor Ellen is shaking like a leaf before she goes on. And I don't know what will happen if our audience gets wind of it.'

'We'll see what we can do,' I said, in as soothing a manner as I could muster.

'I hope you will,' said Selina, and with a final, severe

look she swept out, her cape flying behind her.

Katherine and I sipped our tea reflectively for a few moments. Then Katherine put her cup down, and sighed. 'There's just so much to do,' she said.

'I know,' I replied. 'It's the worst time of year to start delving into whatever shenanigans are going on at the Merrymakers.'

'You're absolutely right,' said Katherine. 'I wouldn't be surprised if it turned out to be one of Mr Templeton's schemes, to pull in audiences.'

'I hadn't thought of that,' I said. 'But you're absolutely right. People love a ghost story at Christmas, don't they?'

Katherine's eyes glinted green, and a dreamy smile curved her lips. 'A ghost story at Christmas,' she murmured.

'But you're right,' I said. 'It could well be one of Mr Templeton's bright ideas. If it is, it should be quite easy to solve.'

'Indeed,' said Katherine, breaking off another piece of her bun. She had got it halfway to her mouth when her hand froze in mid-air. 'If trickery were going on, James would be sure to spot it. With his magician's skills, he could detect any sleight of hand or special effects that Mr T has rigged up.' She popped the morsel of bun in her mouth and chewed with a look of extreme satisfaction.

'It would do Albert good to have a distraction from work,' I said decidedly. 'The new Christmas confectionery Fraser's are launching seems to take up all his time.' I glanced at Katherine, her face now wearing an expression of barely suppressed mischief. 'Are you thinking what I'm thinking, Miss Caster?'

Katherine grinned. 'I'm not a mind reader, Miss Fleet, but I strongly suspect that I am.' She drained her cup and set it down in her saucer with a clack. 'Christmas shopping can wait. To the music hall!'

III
Katherine

It seemed only yesterday that Connie and I had first set foot in the Merrymakers to tackle our second-ever case. Back then, we'd been nervous and a little shocked. Now we sat in our favourite box, bellowing the songs and laughing at the jokes with the rest of the audience, like the regulars we were.

I giggled and Connie looked at me. 'What is it?'

'This afternoon I was ready to drop, and now I'm excited.'

She raised her eyebrows. 'By the pantomime, or the possibility of a mystery?'

'Definitely the first,' I admitted. 'But partly the second, too.'

'If it *is* a case.' Connie smoothed the skirts of her pretty pink dress. I was always a little wistful that my red hair meant I couldn't really wear such a colour, but it suited Connie so well that I didn't feel a bit jealous. I simply wished she'd realise that she always looked every bit a princess.

'True,' I replied. 'Let's be honest, though, Selina is more likely to believe in a talking cat than a ghost. There must be something going on, or she'd never have approached us.'

Connie frowned. 'It'll be one of Mr T's money-making ploys.'

'But Selina could sniff that out in half a minute. Anyway, here goes.'

The conductor tapped the music stand with his baton and the audience fell silent.

'You watch this end of the stage,' said Connie, 'and I'll watch the other.'

'Shh,' said James. 'Stop nattering, you two.'

The orchestra burst into the overture, weaving from lively tune to sad song to waltz to march, then settled into a soft background melody as the curtain rose to reveal a castle kitchen, including a massive stone fireplace with a cauldron. A petite woman in peasant attire stood on a stool with her back to us, pretending to dust the top of the mantelpiece. When she jumped down and faced the audience, we saw that her face and clothes were daubed with what appeared to be soot.

She cast the feather duster into the wings, seized a broom, and swept the floor while singing her first song.

My stepma makes me clean it all
I'm such a grubby mess
I can't go to Prince Charming's ball
Cos I haven't got a dress.

Oh!
I'm poor little Cinderella
I'm working day and night
How can I find a fella
When I look a perfect fright?

I sat enthralled as the pantomime progressed. Mr Templeton had brought off a masterpiece, mixing together risqué jokes, magic and acrobatics, rousing songs for the audience to sing along with, and sentimental ballads to bring a tear to your eye. It was hard not to be entranced, but I concentrated nevertheless, watching for anything amiss.

Cinderella's stepsisters flaunted their hideous party frocks and pushed her away for Buttons to comfort. Then, after Cinderella and Buttons had sung a song together in front of the curtain, it rose to reveal a ballroom so sparkly and golden that it would have made the Palace of Versailles look dreary.

Tilda Golightly, the new actress playing Prince Charming, bounded onto the stage, her well-shaped legs covered only with tights. She was dressed in a thigh-length coat, shiny buckled shoes and a tricorne hat, and she waltzed alone around the ballroom as she bemoaned in song the impossible task of finding a girl to marry. The audience sang along, with a few whistles from some of the men which Tilda ignored entirely. But as she waltzed, one of the mirrors started to tip. Tilda was clearly a professional, making the tiniest stumble before whirling to another part of the stage while a footman hastily steadied the mirror. It was only when she took a bow at the end that I saw the tricorne trembling in her hand.

Connie nudged me when Selina almost tripped over a football which had rolled across the stage. Selina turned it into a joke, pretending the ball was a crystal ball. 'Oooh,' she stage-whispered, peering at it. 'Who's gonna win the cup this year?'

'Clapham Rovers!' shouted someone in the audience.

'Garn then, you help them,' said Selina, throwing him the ball. 'I got things to do.' She swaggered towards Cinderella as if it had all been scripted.

'That was close,' whispered Connie. 'If she hadn't noticed it in time, she could have had a nasty fall.'

The first act drew to a close. Encouraged by Buttons, and with the help of alarming flashes and bangs, the Fairy Godmother transformed Cinders from smut-covered drab to a lady resplendent in eighteenth-century dress, with skirts nearly as wide as Ellen was tall. At one point, after a bit of a hunt, the fairy godmother extracted from the cauldron a golden wig that almost doubled Ellen's height, to chuckles from the audience.

I was so engrossed that I was half over the edge of the box when a pumpkin and some toy mice were somehow magicked into a coach and horses. The accompanying flash and bang made me jump and squeak.

'Careful!' exclaimed James, grabbing me around the waist. 'You nearly fell. The people down there thought you were going to flatten them.'

With as much dignity as I could manage, I pushed his hands away.

'Shh,' whispered Connie. 'Listen.'

At first I couldn't work out what she was talking about. The coach squeaked as it rolled across the floor, while the orchestra played a triumphant march. Behind us, James was destroying the illusions by explaining to Albert how they worked. And then I heard it: a strange, uncanny sound that made my skin crawl. From our vantage point, I saw Selina turn towards the wings for a second, then flick us a glance.

'What's that?' I said.

'What's what?' said Albert.

'That wailing.'

'Wheels need oiling on that carriage,' James said, nodding knowledgeably as he filled his pipe.

I shivered as the noise came again, as grating as a piece of blunt chalk on a slate.

'It's only a sound effect,' sniggered James. 'Come on, Albert, let's get the ladies some refreshments.'

'James is right,' said Albert. 'It'll be someone offstage scratching something to make a sound like squeaky wheels. It's very effective. A certain journalist ought to write this up for the paper.'

'Maybe it's one of the chorus with a sore throat,' said James. They chuckled as they left the box.

The noise had ceased as the curtain fell for the interval, and the audience was milling about. Most were laughing or chatting, but one or two were pointing in the direction from which the strange noise had come. I followed their gaze, and in the darkness at the edge of the stage I saw a figure wrapped in a long robe. The next moment it was gone. 'Did you see that figure, Connie?'

'Just,' Connie replied. 'I think we'll have to delay that shopping trip for a day or two, don't you? The Merrymakers needs us.'

Connie

I awoke with a jolt and smothered a shriek.

'Sorry,' said Albert, 'but you were making a terrible noise. Were you having a nightmare?'

I let out a slow breath. 'Not exactly.'

In my dream, Katherine and I were running along Oxford Street with Mr Templeton and the robed figure from the night before in hot pursuit. Our skirts and fashionable boots hampered us considerably, and people were pushing gift-wrapped boxes at us and rolling footballs in our way, so that we had to dodge them. I looked over my shoulder. The mysterious figure had pulled ahead of Mr Templeton, and its hand was reaching for me. *I'm not having this*, I thought. I wheeled round and grasped the hood which shrouded the figure's face—

And that, of course, was when Albert woke me. I thumped a dent in my pillow and settled back down, but sleep would not come. After a while, I began to make a list in my head of everybody I ought to buy a present for, and felt myself drifting off nicely…

'Good morning, sleepyhead,' said Albert.

I opened an eye to see him tying his cravat. 'What time is it?' I murmured.

'A quarter to nine,' he replied composedly. 'I would have woken you, but after your upset in the night I thought it best to leave you sleeping. Anyway, you're on holiday now. No work for you.'

I blinked. 'I didn't think it was work for you, either,' I replied. 'Today isn't a Fraser's day, is it?'

Albert grimaced. 'At the moment, every day is a Fraser's day. For some reason Mr Fraser has decided I'm the only person he can trust in the successful launch of our Christmas sweets.' He sighed. 'I have inspected foil and cellophane in every colour of the rainbow, and judged the appeal of boxes of all shapes and sizes, and frankly there are days when I could cheerfully never eat a sweet again.'

'I wondered why you'd been refusing pudding,' I commented. 'I thought it was unlike you.'

'I shall make an exception for the Christmas pudding, of course,' said Albert. 'Until then I may confine my consumption of sweet things to those I am compelled to eat by Mr Fraser.' He inspected himself in the mirror and nodded. 'Enjoy your day, Connie.'

'I shall,' I responded, but already my heart was sinking. I wasn't remotely ready for Christmas, and I saw myself imprisoned by piles of irregularly shaped gifts, all of which, for some unknown reason, I would have to wrap. 'The only way to face your fear, Connie, is to confront it,' I told myself sternly, and poured a cup of tea from the breakfast tray. It was lukewarm at best, but I needed something before facing the day.

***

My intention had been to get through the business of the household first thing, then make myself a list of suggested gifts for family and friends, and sally forth. Those tasks completed, a light lunch out would set me up nicely for a cosy chat with Katherine in the office at two o'clock, followed perhaps by a proper afternoon tea.

However, fate had other ideas. As I left the breakfast room I came face to face with Bettina, the nursery-maid we had engaged as a replacement for Lily. 'I'm terribly sorry to bother you, ma'am,' she said, blushing, 'but might I speak to you for a moment?'

'Yes, of course,' I said automatically. Then I thought again. 'Could it wait until Nanny Laidlaw returns from her day off?' I had given our nanny a holiday to go Christmas shopping, since most of her presents would be posted to Scotland.

'I have mentioned the matter to her, but it's rather difficult—'

I re-opened the door of the breakfast room. 'I have a few minutes,' I said.

'It's just that Miss Bee won't talk to me,' said Bettina, looking both confused and embarrassed. 'I'm not sure what to do about it. Nanny Laidlaw said it was probably a phase.' She stood, hands clasped tightly in front of her, her bottom lip trembling. 'I don't think she likes me.'

'Nonsense,' I said. 'I'm sure that isn't it. I shall come to the nursery and have a word with Miss Beatrix, and tell her that she must be more polite.'

Bettina hung her head. 'Thank you, ma'am,' she whispered.

Having gone upstairs to address a mutinous Bee, I found myself drawn into a conversation with Miss Dandridge, the governess, concerning what Bee really ought to be learning by now. Suitably daunted, I played with George and Lydia to cheer myself up, until I was recalled to a sense of what I should be doing by the nursery clock striking midday.

'Oh dear,' I murmured, getting to my feet. 'I had such plans for this morning.'

***

I arrived at the office at five minutes to two. Perhaps it was my mood, but it seemed particularly cheerless without the tree and the paper chains. I filled the kettle and put it on the gas ring, and only then remembered that we had no milk.

I had almost finished my cup of strong black tea when Katherine arrived. 'What time do you call this?' I asked, raising my eyebrows at the clock.

'A quarter past two,' Katherine replied. 'Why, what do you call it?' Then she huffed out a sigh. 'I'm sorry I'm late. The telephone rang just as I was leaving, and – well…'

'Is everything all right?' I asked. 'There's tea in the pot, if you like.'

Katherine took off her hat and coat and hung them on the rack. 'I hope so,' she said. 'It was Thirza. She's a bit worried about Father, but I daresay it's nerves.' Her face, however, told me a different story. 'I'm afraid I can't stay long, as she's asked me to tea, and under the circumstances I couldn't put her off.'

'Don't worry,' I said. 'You have to put your family first. Perhaps we can catch up later.'

'Yes, perhaps,' Katherine said, pouring herself a cup of tea. 'Anyway, how are you?'

'I have an overworked husband, a daughter who won't talk, and no Christmas presents bought whatsoever.' I held out my cup for a refill. 'In the circumstances, the Merrymakers is a pleasant diversion.'

'Indeed,' said Katherine. 'What are your thoughts about last night?'

'I'm really not sure,' I said. 'A lot of it could have been coincidence. Props do come loose, things get onto the stage that shouldn't, and you do sometimes hear noises off and catch glimpses of people in the wings.'

'Yes,' said Katherine. 'But not all in the same night.'

'True.' I remembered the figure in the wings. None of the cast had worn a robe like that at any point during the performance. 'Who could the person in the robe have been?'

Katherine opened the desk drawer and took out a sheet of paper. 'Let's think about who it couldn't have been. Who was on stage when we saw that figure?'

We soon had a list of half a dozen names.

'I would say the person was perhaps my height,' I said. 'So, five feet ten inches. While they could have worn heeled shoes, or stooped, I think the person was between around five feet seven and six feet tall.'

'Good point,' said Katherine, adding more names to the list. 'We could ask Selina for a complete cast list.'

'Don't forget the backstage staff,' I said.

'Yes,' said Katherine, scribbling a note. 'That figure is the key to the mystery.' She tapped her pencil on her teeth. 'What could that weird shrieking noise have been?'

I shivered at the memory of the eldritch squealing. 'I have no idea. And I'm worried about that mirror coming loose. That could have hurt Miss Golightly if she hadn't been so professional.'

Katherine held my gaze. 'You don't think she knew, do you?' She paused. 'I saw her hand shaking afterwards, but that could mean that she'd misjudged, perhaps, and only just saved herself.'

'You could say the same about Selina and the football,' I countered. 'But if she were in on it, she would never have come to us.'

Katherine sighed. 'So far, we have a mysterious robed figure who could be any number of people, a peculiar noise, and a few minor incidents which may or may not be connected.' She studied her sheet of paper, then pushed it away. 'It isn't looking good, is it?'

'We've just begun the investigation,' I said. 'I'm sure we've had less to go on before now.'

'Maybe,' said Katherine. 'If you don't mind, I'll go. It took me a while to get a cab earlier, and Thirza will worry if I'm late.'

'Of course,' I said. 'I hope everything turns out to be all right.'

'So do I,' said Katherine, and her mouth was set in a

firm line as she jammed her hat on her head.

I remained in the office, staring at the sheet of paper. *Can I make sense of it?* But not three minutes later, the door flew open and Katherine hurried towards me. 'I don't believe it,' she muttered, and dropped a newspaper on the desk.

I read the headline, blinked, and looked again.

EXCLUSIVE! CASTER AND FLEET INVESTIGATE HAUNTED THEATRE

V

Katherine

I'll talk to Connie later, I thought, as my cab rattled through the busy London streets. The words of the newspaper article rang in my head all the way to Fulham. If only some minor royal had misbehaved and kept us off the front page…

Should the Merrymakers' Cinderella worry about more than a glass slipper at the witching hour? The theatre may be magical, but this Christmas something ghostly is afoot at one of London's favourite music halls. Reports of strange noises, half-seen visitors and misplaced props are bringing fear to our favourite thespians and their loyal audience. Can Caster and Fleet save the day? Or are our intrepid lady detectives putting themselves in danger of a supernatural kind?

It was hard not to remember Connie's original suggestion that this was a publicity stunt. After all, while fear of ghosts might deter some theatre-goers, it would positively encourage others. But still, something wasn't right about the whole thing.

At half past three, I was ushered into the warm drawing room of my childhood home and embraced my stepmother Thirza.

'I'm so glad you came,' she said, then dropped her voice to a whisper. 'I utterly loathe the *instrument*.' She always spoke of the telephone as if it were a sort of monster. I would have laughed, except that the soft kindliness of her face was marred by a deep frown.

'What is it?' I asked. 'Father's not unwell, is he?'

Thirza's frown deepened. 'I don't *think* so, but—'

'Start at the beginning,' I said. 'Tell me what's worrying you.'

Thirza glanced round the room as if Father might suddenly emerge from the clutter. This was quite possible. It was the same cosy, muddled place it had always been, made more so by the collection of items which Thirza had brought with her on their marriage.

'It began a few weeks ago,' she said. 'He keeps – *forgetting things*. In the last week he's left his umbrella at a restaurant and his muffler at the British Museum. He always tells me not to worry, goes back to retrieve them, and returns safe and well. And it's nice to have a little time to myself. Oh dear, that sounds terribly rude—'

I chuckled. I imagined an occasional break from Father's enthusiasms might be rather welcome.

'But it's unlike him,' said Thirza. 'Especially when it's so cold. I really started to worry when he forgot his hat. He's almost never without a hat. He even wears a nightcap in bed. With tassels.' She giggled and blushed a deep pink that made me squirm a little. 'I mean, you know how formal he is.'

I nodded. My father, while somewhat unconventional in many aspects, was extremely conventional in dress. 'Perhaps he was distracted by his latest venture,' I said. 'What is he working on?'

'A series of Christmas lectures on supernatural folklore. He's been shutting himself away in the study, though all he's had to do is remind himself of his travels and make a few notes.' She pulled a face. 'The study is in rather a mess. But it's not that. Normally he tells me everything he's doing, whether I want to know or not. And he's hardly said a word about these lectures. It's very unlike him to be so secretive.'

The door opened and the maid came in with a loaded tray. 'Shall I fetch the master from the study, ma'am?'

'Don't worry,' I said. 'I'll do it.'

I found Father fast asleep behind a huge pile of books, a red velvet smoking cap obscuring one eye, and surrounded by pieces of paper covered in scribbles.

'Hello, Father,' I said loudly, making him jerk awake. 'Tea's waiting.'

'Ah, Kitty.' He blinked and peered round the pile of books at me. 'How lovely. Have you brought the little fellow?'

Although Father would have liked Ed to spend more time sitting still and listening to him read stories, and less time running around and being noisy, nothing made him happier than pulling faces, telling silly jokes and singing nonsense songs out of tune, to Ed's immense delight.

'Not this time,' I said. 'But we'll have the train journey to Berkshire together on Christmas Eve.'

A thoughtful expression crossed Father's face. 'I was wondering whether to dress up as Father Christmas and surprise him.'

I considered this idea. 'He's too young, and he might be frightened. Next year, perhaps.'

'Talking of frightening—' Father pulled a newspaper from the pile of clutter. I saw the headline and felt myself blanch. Then I realised he was opening it to the events section, and remembered that I had never been sure whether he knew that Caster and Fleet were actually me and Connie. 'I hope you'll come to my lectures. I'll be speaking about how peasants from all around the world recount strange and sinister events in folklore. You've always been rather sensible, and not especially interested in mysteries, but you might enjoy these.'

'The mystery I'm most interested in is why you left the muffler I gave you for your birthday at the British Museum.'

Father grimaced. 'Thirza does fuss so. When one is engaged in the creative process, one cannot waste time on the mundane.'

'At least she cares,' I said. 'You shouldn't make her worry because you're wrapped up in your own interests.'

'Yes, dear,' he answered. 'Now, about my first lecture. You'll never guess…'

***

'It was a complete waste of time,' I told Connie two hours later. 'Father seemed quite as normal, for him. Thirza was worrying unnecessarily.'

'Perhaps that's not so strange,' said Connie. 'It's only a few years since she had all that trouble. And in midwinter, when it's dark, her nerves tend to get the better of her.'

'I know.' I sighed. 'But I shouldn't have left you to work on the case alone. If it is one.' I told her my doubts.

To my surprise, she frowned. 'What is it?' I asked.

'When you left, I thought maybe doing something else would clear my mind, so I went shopping. It needs doing, after all.' She fell silent and fiddled with her rings.

'Was shopping so terrible?' I prompted. I knew this wasn't about presents.

Connie shrugged. 'I went to Oxford Street and Regent Street. It was busy and very dark, apart from the lights. Albert would be rather cross to know I was wandering alone, and Mother would be frankly appalled, but I really must finish my shopping. Or should I say, start it.' She sighed again.

'Go on.'

'I wandered round Liberty's for ages – they have such pretty things – then went down Regent Street and had a look in Hamley's to see if I could find any presents for the children. Not that Bee deserves anything at the moment, but that's beside the point.'

'What is the point?' I said.

'I felt as if someone were watching me. It was such an odd sensation. Everything Mother's ever said about ladies walking alone came into my head. Then I remembered you and I have been in much more dangerous situations than Christmas shopping in Regent Street, and pulled myself together. But I could have sworn I was being followed by a short man in a huge coat and a massive muffler, with a bowler hat on top.'

I smiled. 'Maybe he's got Father's muffler.'

Connie seemed not so much frightened as puzzled. 'It wasn't his style,' she said. 'Quite the wrong colour. Anyway, as I say, I kept seeing this man. I told myself it couldn't be the same one, as men tend to all dress the same, but I'm sure it was. Then I realised I was being absurd. I daresay he's at home right this moment, complaining about a tall woman who kept following him and staring at him in Regent Street *and* Oxford Street, when really we're just two people feeling fraught because we've left our Christmas shopping late.'

I gave her a hug. 'We're both being absurd,' I said. 'The first mention of ghosts and we're imagining things. What we need to solve this case is someone who knows how these things work from the inside.'

Connie eyed me. 'You think we should take the case.'

'I do. Don't you?'

Connie nodded. 'And I know exactly who to ask for help.'

VI Connie

'Oh yes, I'm ready for Christmas,' said Tina. 'Everything is bought and wrapped, Cook will take care of the food, and I've done all my Mrs Minchin advice columns until January. I fully intend to put my feet up and enjoy myself.' She studied us over the rim of her cup. 'That is, unless you have other ideas.'

Katherine and I exchanged glances, then stared at Tina as she began to giggle. 'Bless the pair of you,' she said. 'Don't you think I read the papers? I did wonder, when I saw you two on the front page, how long it would be before I heard from you.' I looked at Tina – Mrs Ernestine Hamilton, as she now was – splendid in teal silk in her Bayswater drawing room, and remembered the first time I had met her, in a black wig, as Bassalissa the fortune-teller.

'We wouldn't want to impose,' I said, faintly. 'It's just that we've been so busy, and Christmas has rushed up on us, rather.'

'Even though it comes at the same time every year,'

Tina said drily.

'The Christmas part is fine,' I said. 'It's the unpredictable behaviour of families that makes things difficult.'

'Mmm,' said Tina. 'I know about that from my postbag. Anyway.' She put her cup down. 'From what I've read there are odd goings-on at the Merrymakers, including a mysterious hooded figure, unearthly noises, and general mishaps. Is that true, or are the journalists enjoying themselves?'

'It's true,' said Katherine. 'We were at a performance and all those things happened. Including the figure. James could explain the magic tricks, but not the other things. Some of it could have been coincidence—'

'But not all of it, eh?' Tina clasped her hands under her chin and sat for a while, thinking. 'As I said, I'm ready for Christmas and I plan to enjoy myself. Now, Tilly's school hasn't broken up yet, and she's rather cross. A trip to the Saturday matinee might be a nice little pick-me-up. If it is someone having a joke, I doubt they'll do too much in the daytime when children are there, whereas a supernatural personage wouldn't bother about that, if you catch my drift. And Tilly's got sharp eyes, just like her ma. Between us, if there's something to be seen, I reckon we'll see it.'

'Thank you so much, Tina,' I said. 'That really is a weight off my mind.'

'Not a problem,' said Tina. 'Interesting that you were clocked at the music hall though, wasn't it? Almost as if someone was watching out for you. Then again, a pair of ladies as . . . as—'

'I suppose we are quite well-known,' I said, hoping I wasn't blushing.

Tina smiled. 'I was looking for the word conspicuous,' she said. 'But well-known too, of course. That's one of the reasons why I've always kept myself to myself – specially when I was Bassalissa. I like to go about my business nice and quietly.'

'So do we!' I said, indignantly. 'And we were, until our last big case.'

'I was only teasing,' said Tina. 'It's no penance to spend an afternoon with my daughter at the music hall. I'll get in touch afterwards and tell you what we saw.'

'Thank you, Tina.' As Katherine and I rose to take our leave, I decided to ask the question that had been on my mind for most of our short visit. 'Tell me, how are you prepared for Christmas already?'

Tina grinned. 'That's easy, I started in January. I've been squirrelling things away all year. And I wrote my Christmas cards in November.'

'I see,' I replied, thinking that I would rather have a flurry in December than spread Christmas thinly over a whole year, as if trying to get a small quantity of butter right to the edges of a large piece of toast.

'Do you think she's right?' Katherine asked, as Tredwell drove the short distance to her house. 'Will whoever or – whatever it is behave differently at the matinee?'

'Who knows,' I replied. 'But if there's anything to be seen, Tina will see it.' I imagined her sitting at her desk in November, with a roaring fire and a pot of tea at her elbow, methodically writing Christmas cards, and sighed. *Time to tackle Christmas, Connie.*

***

I arrived home full of good intentions. I took off my coat, unpinned my hat, and gave them both to Johnson, who looked perturbed. 'Is everything all right?' I asked.

'Oh yes, ma'am, I'm sure it is. Er, Nanny Laidlaw wondered if you would do her the favour of paying a visit to the nursery when it is convenient.'

'Oh.' Nanny Laidlaw was wonderful, efficient, and adored by the children. I nevertheless found her rather frightening. 'I don't suppose Albert is at home,' I speculated.

'Oh yes, ma'am, he is in the study, though I believe he is going out later.'

'In that case I shall go to him first, then attend to Nanny,' I said firmly.

The study door opened and Albert strolled into the hall. 'Did someone mention my name in vain?' he said, smiling, and kissed me on the cheek. 'Must dash, Connie, confectionery calls.'

'Again?' I followed him to the front door. 'I'm starting to think you should set up a camp bed at the factory.'

Albert laughed. 'It isn't quite that bad, Connie. Soon it will be out of our hands. It launches in three days' time, you know.'

'What launches?' I demanded. 'Here you are spending all this time at Fraser's, and I don't even know what it's for!'

'Three days, Connie,' Albert replied, with maddening

calm.

'Ah, Mrs Lamont.'

The voice came from the landing above my head. It had a faint Scottish inflection. 'Good afternoon, Nanny Laidlaw,' I said, not without dread.

'I wonder if I might speak to you for a moment,' Nanny Laidlaw said, gliding down the stairs.

'Of course,' I replied, and took Albert's arm so that he could not get away. Johnson took one look at the advancing figure and sped towards his own quarters.

'It concerns Miss Bee. Young Bettina had mentioned something about her not speaking the other day. At the time I dismissed it as a bit of fancy on one or both of their parts. However, since I returned from my day off, Miss Bee is refusing to speak to me, too. I have of course reprimanded her for this behaviour, but she remains stubbornly silent.'

'That's odd,' I said. 'I have spoken to her myself about this, and she knows it's naughty.'

'I expect it's just a phase,' said Albert, and both Nanny Laidlaw and I turned to him in surprise. 'I'm sure she'll get tired of it soon. But I don't think you should punish her.'

Nanny Laidlaw's eyebrows almost disappeared behind her cap. 'Very well, sir,' she said. 'As you wish.' She swept back upstairs.

'You can let go of me now,' said Albert. 'Honestly, Connie.'

We both jumped at a loud knock on the door. 'What now?' said Albert, as Johnson scurried past us to answer it.

He opened the door to reveal a short, stout man in a bowler hat and a suit of rather a loud check. 'Roger Hammersley Esquire, of the *Bugle*,' he said, producing a card. 'Might I speak to—'

'I don't believe it,' breathed Albert. 'We've been so careful, and some rotter has spilled the beans!'

Mr Hammersley looked at him without much interest. 'I'm sure I don't know what you mean, sir. I wondered if I might have a word with your good lady wife.' He turned to me, doffed his hat, and made a low bow. 'If you are, as I believe, the illustrious Miss Fleet, I would greatly value the opportunity to speak with you about the strange phenomenon at the Merrymakers Music Hall. Could I possibly have a few moments of your time?'

'Whatever is it?' I cried as Thirza was ushered without prior warning into my sitting room on Saturday afternoon.

'I'm so sorry,' she said. 'But I'm more worried than ever.'

'Honestly, Thirza, it's just Father deep in one of his ideas again.'

She twisted her gloves almost into a knot. 'I'm still not convinced. I don't know how to tell you what I've done. I —' She rummaged for a lacy handkerchief and dabbed her eyes.

'Go on,' I encouraged. 'I can't believe you've done anything so terrible.'

'I feel as if I have,' she said. 'I don't know how you and James manage money affairs but I'm old-fashioned and leave everything to Roderick. Even if I want something from my own account, I ask him to help. I really don't like banks.' Thirza lifted her capacious handbag into her lap and started to forage.

At that moment Ed burst in trailing his toy dog Patch, followed by his nursemaid Gwen who gave me an apologetic look. 'Gamma!' he cried, and clambered onto Thirza's lap, knocking the handbag on the floor, where its contents spilled all over the carpet. Thirza cuddled him, but gave me an agonised glance.

Gwen stooped to pick up Thirza's things. 'Don't worry, I'll do that,' I said. 'Can you help Ed give Patch his tea?'

Gwen was more than used to stopping Ed from interrupting a client. If she was surprised that this time it was my stepmother, she made no sign. 'Come along, Master Ed. I think Patch should choose some biscuits, don't you?'

Once they'd left, I knelt and retrieved the things that had fallen out of Thirza's handbag. The last item was a bank book in Father's name. 'Is this what you're talking about?'

'Yes,' said Thirza. 'The day he went to retrieve his muffler, I was looking among the chaos on his desk in case it was there. The book was open and I – I couldn't help it. I know it'll make you uncomfortable, but it's important that you see.'

It certainly did make me uncomfortable, but I sat alongside her and flipped through the pages. Father had a fixed income from investments, to which he added what he earned from book sales, articles and lectures. He was frugal, withdrawing the same amount every week, some of which he would pass to Thirza for the housekeeping expenses.

The book covered three years. Father had behaved with

complete regularity until two weeks ago, when he had withdrawn £150. I gasped. 'Does the house need a new roof?' I asked. Not that I could imagine a roof costing so much.

Thirza shook her head. 'It occurred just when he started losing things. You—' Her voice trembled. 'You don't suppose he's set up a second household with somebody else?'

'No!' I exclaimed, putting my arms round her. 'Father adores you. Did anything else happen at that time?'

Thirza dabbed her eyes again. 'I'm sure he had some foreign letters. What if he saw something untoward when he travelled abroad investigating folklore? Could it be blackmail? Or…' And now Thirza really did look worried.

I went cold inside. 'Or what? Tell me, Thirza.'

'He got so involved in research for his lectures that he met with some spiritualists. People who do seances, and so on. Weren't you caught up in something similar a few years ago?'

Now I was worried too. Father's conviction that everyone was as honest as he was could be his undoing.

'What does he say about it?'

'I can't ask!' She sniffled. 'He'd think I didn't trust him.'

I gave her another hug. 'You and Father are coming for Sunday lunch tomorrow. I promise to find out what's going on.'

Ed returned and climbed into Thirza's lap, where he pretended to feed Patch biscuits while covering everything with crumbs. I forced a smile. I wished I felt as confident as I pretended to be.

The telephone bell was a relief at first, but Connie's voice was agitated. 'Can you get away?' she said. 'Tina says that some of the audience were genuinely scared by the eerie goings-on. We must speak to Mr Templeton because if this is a publicity stunt, it's got completely out of hand. If we could get to the Merrymakers before the evening performance begins—'

'Thirza's here,' I answered. 'But it'll cheer her up to play with Ed till James comes home. I'll see you shortly.'

***

Mr Templeton didn't seem entirely pleased to see us. However, we'd both long since stopped being daunted by his bluster.

'Once you two get involved, everything always goes to pot! Today a load o' mothers asked for their money back. I know the evening sales are up, but that don't mean I want to lose out on the matinee. Then I sprains me ankle and the understudy 'as to take over, and I—'

'How did you sprain your ankle?' asked Connie.

'Don't you start,' Mr Templeton snapped. 'It weren't no ghost if that's what you're hinting at. It weren't even here at the theatre, it was the bottom step at home what done it. And the understudy's good, but he ain't as good as me. Besides, I like dressing up.' He repeated the hip-wiggle he used when flirting with Prince Charming, then winced as his ankle gave way.

'Christmas ghost stories are all the rage at the moment,' I said. 'But Cinderella is a pantomime.'

'I dunno what mothers are coming to. I never got

mollycoddled like those little—'

I thought of Ed and lost my temper. 'You may be as sensitive as a brick, but it isn't fair to frighten children because some people want the thrill of saying they've been to a haunted theatre!'

'Here, hang on!' Mr Templeton lunged forward and winced again. 'The kids were wailing to stay! It was their mothers causing the fuss. What you accusing me of? You think I set this up?'

'It certainly looks that way,' said Connie. 'You've always known how to draw a good audience.'

'You—' Mr Templeton forced a cigar into his mouth so hard that he nearly swallowed it. 'I'm a showman, not a conman!' He gave us both a hard stare. 'Right, we three will watch the show from beginning to end, in the special box. You tell me what you see, and I'll tell you what's actually happening. I'm not having you two accuse me of being a trickster.'

He herded us before him as he limped along, muttering under his breath. I wasn't sure if he was swearing about us or his ankle.

At first, nothing seemed untoward at all. Mr Templeton settled back in his chair with his arms folded, the offending foot raised on a low stool. 'Garn then, what's wrong?' he growled. 'Where's this ghost?'

I exchanged glances with Connie. Everything had begun normally the other evening, too. But the performers, who had appeared nervous to begin with, started to relax and enjoy themselves. The understudy didn't have the aplomb – or girth – of Mr Templeton, but he made the performance his own, wiggling his crinoline, winking his monstrous eyelashes, and blowing kisses at the men in the front row to cheers and whistles.

I wanted to laugh, too. I wanted to relax like the actors, but I couldn't. I told myself that I was disturbed by the conversation with Thirza, and worried about Connie, but this was different: a creeping sensation that something would happen when I least expected it.

'Still nothing.' Mr Templeton lit another cigar and waved it at the stage. 'Here comes my new acquisition. What you think of Tilda, eh? I'm not sure if we'll make her name or she'll make ours, but either way, she's a find.'

Miss Golightly strode on stage and slapped her slender thigh as she declaimed Prince Charming's opening words. 'Are there any beautiful girls in this place?'

As before, several female voices in the audience cried, 'Yes! Me!' and other voices responded, 'Garn! Not in Lambeth!'

The orchestra struck up a gentle waltz and Miss Golightly began her lonely dance, pirouetting round the ballroom as she sang:

Will I be always so alone, alone?
Will I never bring a bride home, back home?
So rich and yet so poor,
Without a true love to adore.

She hesitated as she approached the mirror which had once nearly fallen, but all that happened was that her reflection sparkled as it should. Then she spun to the next mirror.

It took a second or two to realise what was wrong. The mirror didn't move, it didn't even wobble, but the figure in the mirror was not Prince Charming's reflection. It was a tall figure in a black robe.

With a terrified scream, Miss Golightly ran to the front of the stage and jumped off. The audience, confused and unnerved, stood up in consternation, blocking Tilda's way as she desperately sought the exit.

For an injured man, Mr Templeton moved with remarkable speed. 'You two, go and get Tilda. And when you find her, tell her there's nothing to worry about.'

'Where are you going?' asked Katherine.

'To call an early interval, and sort out this mess,' retorted Mr Templeton. A second later, the door of the box banged behind him.

Katherine and I looked at each other. 'If he's sorting it out, he must know what's going on,' I said.

Katherine opened the door. 'So what are we waiting for?'

The volume of chatter rose as we left the box and hurried first down the corridor, then downstairs. A small man in a muffler and a bowler hat – Roger Hammersley, I suspected – scurried through the foyer and left, and from within the auditorium Mr Templeton bellowed, 'Interval! Get your refreshments at the bar! Move along now!' But our eyes were fixed on a slim figure in breeches confronting Ron, the box-office manager and general assistant, who was barring the nearest exit.

'I won't stay here a minute longer!' she bawled, in an accent markedly different from the one we had heard on stage. 'First you lot try to crush me with a mirror, then you scare me to death! I ain't having it!'

'You should be telling Mr Templeton that, not me,' said Ron, but he looked very nervous.

'I don't care!' screeched Tilda, in a voice that would have carried to the back of the upper circle. 'Mr Templeton can take his job and shove it up his—'

'Miss Golightly!' I cried, hurrying over and touching her arm. 'I'm so glad to meet you at last. I am Miss Fleet, of the Caster and Fleet Detective Agency.'

Tilda Golightly's mouth dropped open. 'You're Miss Fleet?' She couldn't have stared any harder if I had had two heads. Then she saw Katherine. 'And that's Miss Caster?'

Katherine nodded.

'But you're – you're...' She frowned. 'I didn't think you was real.'

Whatever else I had expected, that wasn't it. 'Of course we're real,' I said, laughing. 'We are investigating the strange things that have been happening.'

'And I've got an explanation,' boomed Mr Templeton, throwing open the double doors which led to the stalls. 'I present to you . . . the mysterious monk!' He stepped aside to reveal a nervous-looking elderly man in a long black robe. 'Or as his congregation know him, Father Francis Ivor of St Mary's Church. I brought him in to see off any evil spirits that might be lurking.'

'I'm terribly sorry if I scared you, Miss Golightly,' said Father Francis, wringing his hands. 'Mr Templeton asked me to remain inconspicuous while I was going about my business, and I have tried my best – hence the cloak – but I must have taken a wrong turning backstage.'

Tilda drew herself up to her full height. 'I see,' she said. 'In that case, I suppose there's no hard feelings.'

'Come and have a drink with me, Tilda,' said Mr Templeton. 'I've got brandy in the office – strictly for medicinal purposes, of course – to strengthen you for the second half.'

Tilda fixed him with a steely eye. 'Two conditions,' she said. 'A pound a week extra for the rest of the run, and no priests hanging around backstage.' She glared at Father Francis, who seemed to have shrunk a foot in the last couple of minutes.

'We'll talk it over, my dear,' said Mr Templeton, in a soothing voice. He gave us a brisk nod, then took Tilda's arm and led her away.

Ron exhaled in a way that suggested he had been holding his breath for some time. 'Well, that was interesting,' he said.

'It explains the hooded figure,' said Katherine. 'But there is still more to work out.'

'Sometimes priests stir up that sort of thing,' said Ron. 'You know, strange phemonny – phenonny – weird stuff. Once he's gone it'll probably quieten down. You wait and see.'

And after the interval, it appeared Ron might be right.

Despite Katherine and I watching carefully, there were no misbehaving props and no strange noises. If anything, the audience seemed rather disappointed. 'I wasn't a *bit* scared,' complained one young woman, as she left on the arm of her beau.

Katherine and I were both quiet as Tredwell drove us over Lambeth Bridge. I studied Katherine, who was gazing out of the window, chin on hand. 'You don't believe it was about the priest either, do you?' I said.

She turned. 'Of course not,' she said. 'It's like what Tina said. When there was a real risk of the show falling apart, the pranks stopped. So it definitely isn't a ghost – not that I ever thought it was,' she added quickly. 'It's someone playing the fool.'

'If that's all it is,' I said, 'we can solve this. But not tonight.'

'I'm glad you said that,' Katherine replied, stifling a huge yawn. 'Telephone me in the morning if you have any bright ideas.'

Once I had dropped Katherine off at her house, I settled back in my seat with a sigh. The case was further forward… *But there is still so much to do.*

I returned home to a quiet house, but Johnson seemed perturbed again. *Whatever it is*, I thought, *I am not equipped to deal with it now*. 'Goodnight, Johnson,' I said, and made for the stairs.

'Excuse me, ma'am—'

Darn! 'What is it, Johnson?' I said, turning.

'Bettina asked me to give you this when you came in, ma'am,' he said, producing a slightly crumpled envelope from his pocket.

I sighed, took it, and ripped it open.

Dear Mrs Lamont,

I am sorry to do this, but I am writing to give notice. You have been very kind to me, but I have found it hard to take care of a child who I am sure does not like me. I will work out my month, of course, and I hope my time in this post, though brief, has been satisfactory.

Yours most sincerely,

Miss Bettina Quimby

I refolded the note and stuffed it into my bag. 'Thank you, Johnson, and goodnight,' I said, and dragged myself up the stairs.

***

Surprisingly, I woke at seven from a deep, dreamless sleep. *Right*, I thought, sitting up in bed, and rang for tea.

'Good heavens,' murmured Albert, rolling over and regarding me with a half-open eye. 'It's Sunday. We needn't be at church till eleven.'

'Indeed,' I said, reaching for my bed-jacket. 'But I have things to resolve first. Bettina gave notice last night.'

'Oh no,' murmured Albert, pinching the bridge of his nose.

'Oh yes,' I said. 'I'll get to the bottom of this situation with Bee if it kills me.'

'I'm not sure that's such a good idea,' said Albert. 'At least wait until you've had breakfast.'

I stared at him. 'What sort of monster do you think I

am? I'm not doing this on an empty stomach.'

An hour later, fortified and dressed, I made my way to the nursery. 'I would like to speak to Miss Bee in private, please,' I announced grandly.

Bettina looked at me with wide, scared eyes, then got up. 'Come, Master Georgie and Miss Lydia,' she said, holding out a hand to both of them. 'Let's go and play in the schoolroom for a little while.'

I lowered myself carefully onto the small chair opposite Bee. 'Beatrix Lamont, explain yourself, if you please.'

Bee faced me, her mouth clamped firmly shut.

'Oh, so you're not speaking to me, either?'

Bee swallowed, and slowly shook her head.

I folded my arms and glared at Bee, for the want of any better ideas, and she glared back at me.

We both looked round at the creak from the nursery door. Albert entered, and took a seat between us. 'Bee,' he said, taking her hand, 'when I told you not to tell anyone, this isn't exactly what I meant.'

Bee's eyes nearly popped out of her head. 'But you said —'

'Not to tell anyone what?' I demanded.

'I heard Papa in his study,' said Bee. 'On the telephone, talking about sweeties.'

'Yes, you did,' said Albert. 'Although you haven't mentioned that you were hiding behind the armchair.'

'Oh, Bee…' I reached over and ruffled her ringlets.

'It happened to be rather a private conversation about sweeties,' said Albert. 'So I made Bee promise not to tell anybody, and gave her one of our new sweets to seal the deal.'

'I haven't even eaten it,' said Bee proudly. 'I put it in my special things box. And I've said nothing to anyone. Specially people I don't really know, like Bettina. And when Nanny Laidlaw wasn't here I thought that was suspicious, so I was careful.'

'Yes, you were,' said Albert. 'But you've upset Bettina. She doesn't understand why you won't speak to her.'

Bee flung up her chin. 'She ought to know some things are private,' she said, tossing her ringlets.

Albert and I exchanged glances. 'I think the best thing to do,' Albert said, 'is to call Bettina and Nanny Laidlaw, explain the situation, and tell them it was all my fault. It doesn't matter now, anyway.'

Bee swelled with indignation until she appeared ready to burst. She looked first at me, then Albert, and finally cried, with explosive fury, 'Grown-ups!'

***

'That went well,' I said to Albert, as we descended the stairs.

'I feel about two inches tall,' he replied. 'There's nothing like being regarded with disdain by three women and one small girl to cut you down to size.'

'You'll get over it,' I said, and laughed.

As we reached the hall the letterbox rattled, and the end of a rolled-up newspaper appeared.

'That's odd,' I said, frowning. 'You've already had your newspapers, haven't you?'

'Oh yes,' said Albert. 'I had the *Times* at breakfast, remember?'

I stepped forward and pulled out the newspaper. 'We haven't started taking the *Sunday Bugle*, have we?'

'I'll have a word with Johnson,' said Albert, holding out his hand for the paper.

But one glance at the front page made the reason for the newspaper's arrival only too clear.

CASTER AND FLEET BAMBOOZLED

TRICKSTER GHOST CAUSES MAYHEM AT MUSIC HALL

It was such a lovely morning that we walked the long way to church, partly in the hope of wearing Ed out and discouraging him from helping the vicar to light the advent candle.

Afterwards Gwen and I took the direct route home to be in plenty of time for Father and Thirza, while James went to buy a newspaper. He burst through the door while I was unbuttoning Ed's coat, nearly bowling us both over, and pushed the *Sunday Bugle* into my hands just as the telephone rang. At the other end of the line, Connie spluttered the same headline I was reading.

'I wish we'd never become involved,' I said. 'It's ridiculous. One moment we are heroines, next moment we're failures.'

'Exactly,' said Connie. 'I'm fed up with it, even though Albert thinks we should plough on. I shall calm my nerves with a good book and a cup of tea and forget everything else.'

'Why don't all of you come for tea this afternoon? Father and Thirza are here for lunch but want to be home before dark, so they aren't staying. The children, Albert and James can distract each other while we talk. And speaking of talking, how's Bee?'

'Ah,' said Connie, and I could hear a tiny smile in her voice. 'That's a story for another time.'

'Don't worry about the papers,' said James, giving me a hearty kiss. 'You two will work it out.'

'What's that strange squelchy noise? There must be something wrong with the line,' said Connie, and hung up.

***

As planned, Father and Thirza arrived early enough for the three of us to take Ed to the park, where Thirza marched him off to see the ducks. 'Ampapa!' he cried, beckoning Father.

'Later,' said Thirza. 'Grandpapa would like to talk to Mother.'

'Would I?' said Father. He pouted. 'You weren't at my talk last night, Kitty. You've missed them all so far.'

'I do intend to come tonight,' I said. 'But never mind that.' How do you ask your father what he's doing with his own money? 'I'll cut to the chase. Thirza is so worried about you that she thinks you've set up a second household.'

Father went purple, then white. 'That's terrible!' he said. 'How could she possibly think that? I never thought I would love another woman after your mother died, but Thirza is everything to me!'

He fell silent and we watched Ed, who was throwing

massive chunks of stale bread to the ducks. It was as well for the ducks that he was mostly throwing them backwards. Father frowned. 'Will you absolutely promise to keep this quiet until Christmas Day?'

'If it's not illegal, of course I shall.'

'Illegal? Whatever has come over you, Kitty? You seem to see mysteries everywhere.'

'You've been behaving strangely for a fortnight,' I replied. 'It's . . . it's nothing to do with a haunted music hall, is it?'

'Whatever would make you think that?' Father scratched his beard, and huffed a sigh. 'It's a present.'

My mouth dropped open.

'It's meant to be a secret,' he continued. 'You see, Thirza has barely been out of London, and the one place I haven't been to is the middle of the Atlantic Ocean. So I've bought us tickets.'

'To the middle of the Atlantic Ocean?'

Father ignored my confusion. 'We're sailing first class to Madeira, staying in one of the best hotels for three months, and coming back at Easter. The warm climate will suit us both. It is rather expensive, but there will still be plenty of money left for you and Margaret when the time comes.'

'Oh, Father!' A lump came to my throat as I remembered all those years when he had been missing, presumed dead. I flung my arms around him. 'Please don't say that. I want you to be driving me mad when I'm an old lady myself. It's a wonderful idea. I can't wait to see Thirza's face on Christmas Day.'

'Good,' said Father. 'Now let's go and rescue those ducks from Ed.'

***

The Lamonts arrived promptly at four. We enjoyed a leisurely tea in the drawing room together before the children went to play in the nursery, while James and Albert went to the study to smoke and talk politics, leaving us in peace.

I gazed into Connie's face. 'You look a lot better.'

'So do you. I take it your discussion with your father was a success. Can you tell me about it?'

'Not yet,' I said, 'but everything's all right. How about you?'

Connie burst into a rich delicious laugh that I hadn't heard for several days. 'I can't tell you everything yet either, but I shall. Now all that's left to sort out is the Merrymakers. Let's start from the beginning. What are your thoughts?'

I pondered. 'A phrase my father said: *everything is obvious when looked at in the right way*. I should have realised that if he were keeping a secret – which isn't like him – but was also quite happy, there must be a simple explanation. It was obvious, in a way.'

Connie nodded. 'The same goes for Bee. I was looking at it from the wrong angle. When I thought about why a child might stop talking, the answers became clear.'

'Perhaps we should apply the same principle to the Merrymakers. We saw that something was wrong and Selina said she was scared, which was odd, since she's a cynic and not naturally nervous. Neither of us thought it was a ghost, did we? But we did somehow catch her apprehension.'

Connie grimaced. 'We picked up on her anxiety rather than considering the situation with logical minds.'

'A theatre is already a place of illusion,' I said slowly. 'And actors can be superstitious and nervous. What better place to make the small and ordinary seem overwhelming? But Mr Templeton isn't a fool. He's experienced enough to know where to draw the line.'

'He seemed both baffled and unnerved,' said Connie. 'I had the impression he brought in the priest to put his own mind at rest, although perhaps he should have warned the cast. I still don't think he's behind it.'

'What else?' I pondered. 'I agree it seems unlike him to risk his takings and the reputation of the music hall.'

'Mmm,' said Connie. 'He was irritated by the mothers asking for their money back, but you could see his ears prick up when he realised people were disappointed that there wasn't a ghost. It was as if a penny dropped and he suddenly saw the potential for the audience to be frightened just the right amount.'

'What about the children?' I argued.

'Mr Templeton said the *children* loved it,' Connie reminded me. 'It was the mothers who made a fuss.' She gave me a stern look and I squirmed, determined I wouldn't turn out the same. 'When I was quite young, I was taken to a performance of *A Christmas Carol*. I was absolutely enthralled throughout and loved the spirits best of all. There's a real place for it if you get it right.'

'Not in Cinderella,' I said.

'But if you're going to have a castle and a palace, you might as well have a ghost,' said Connie. 'I'm surprised Mr Templeton didn't consider it himself. It isn't the West End, it's the Merrymakers Music Hall in Lambeth. Their productions are loud, funny, silly, sentimental, and unpredictable. Why can't they be ghostly too?'

The two of us sat in silence for a bit. Then the children joined us and insisted we watch Bee attempt some of James's conjuring tricks. It was hard to concentrate on them as our minds whirred.

'If you got the ghostly balance wrong, it would be disastrous,' said Connie. 'But if you got it right, it would be absolutely stupendous. I'm sure Mr Templeton isn't behind this.'

'Selina?' I suggested.

'No,' said Connie. 'There's nothing duplicitous about her.'

'Then it must be somebody else. Someone with knowledge, but maybe not subtlety or sophistication.'

Bee palmed a coin. Or at least, she distracted the others by pointing across the room while shoving the penny up her sleeve. Ed and George gasped as they stared at her empty hands. Where had it gone?

'Abracadabrabra!' She 'found' it behind George's ear to crows of amazement.

'Maybe one day she could make a superlative stage magician, with a male assistant being cut in half for a change,' whispered Connie.

'Stupendous? Duplicitous? Superlative? Have you swallowed one of Father's books?' I said. Then Connie and

I looked at each other, and the penny dropped.

'Hocus pocus!' she said. 'Hey presto! I can squeeze in one more visit to the Merrymakers before Christmas, Miss Caster. How about you?'

X
Connie

'When I suggested another trip to the Merrymakers,' I said, in as dignified a manner as I could, 'this wasn't quite what I had in mind.'

'I don't suppose it was,' said Katherine, her voice rather muffled. 'But you have to admit it's a brilliant disguise.'

'It is if you can see properly,' I retorted. 'And I'm very warm.'

'Never mind,' said Katherine. 'Hopefully it won't be for too long.' She sighed. 'I suppose I'd better put my head on now.'

'Yes, why do *I* have to be the back end of the horse?' I demanded.

'Um, because you're too tall to fit in the front half? Ssshh, we're on in a minute.'

Selina had smuggled us in through the stage door half an hour before. It was a sort of closed open secret that we were here; Mr Templeton had informed the whole cast separately, and given them to understand that not everybody knew. He had complained about it afterwards to us, of course, although as he was dressed in his Ugly Sister outfit it was hard to take him seriously.

'I don't see the point of all this skulking around,' he had said, hands on his impossibly wide hips.

'Perhaps it takes a skulker to catch a skulker,' I replied, drawing myself up, centaur-like.

'Hmmm,' said Mr Templeton, pursing his red lips. 'You promise you won't wreck my pantomime?'

'Would we ever do such a thing?' said Katherine.

'I wouldn't put it past you,' Mr Templeton retorted, with a toss of his curly wig.

And now we were in the wings, waiting to go on. With the help of Selina and Tina, we had compiled a list of the points in the pantomime when supernatural intervention seemed most likely. Our plan was to go on and thwart it.

Ellen was on stage alone, dressed in her rags, and about to break into a sad, sad song. 'Oh dear,' she sighed, as she swept the stage.

'Move up a bit,' murmured Katherine. 'I can't get my head on stage.'

I shuffled forward.

'Hello!' Katherine called.

Ellen whipped around. To her credit, her astonishment at being confronted with the head of a pantomime horse seemed entirely genuine. 'Umm . . . you can talk!' she cried.

'Of course I can talk,' Katherine responded. 'This is a pantomime, isn't it?'

'I should say so,' said Ellen. 'But what are you doing

here?'

'I am Dobbin, your father's faithful steed, and I have sworn to protect you, Cinderella. May I come in?'

'I suppose, so long as you don't mess up my nice clean floor,' said Ellen. 'I was just about to sing myself a sad song. Would you like to listen to it?'

'Oh yes, I'd love to.' I felt Katherine sidestep to the right, and followed her. The audience were laughing, so I presumed all was well.

'How I wish Mother were here,' exclaimed Ellen, and began her song.

Then I heard it, even through the body of the horse; a ghastly keening, much louder than it had been before. *EEEOOOEEEOOOUUU!*

Ellen stopped singing and gasped. The band stopped too, and the silence was broken by the exclamations of the audience. Then the wail came again.

'Here goes,' muttered Katherine. 'Someone's left the back door open!' she cried, and set off at a gallop. I lurched behind, holding her waist, unable to see anything apart from occasional glimpses of the stage beneath me from the eyeholes that someone had thoughtfully cut in the horse's belly.

We had just reached the darkness of the wings when Katherine stopped as though she had hit a wall. I crashed into her, and we both fell down.

'Oof!' exclaimed someone who definitely wasn't Katherine.

'It's all right, Connie,' whispered Katherine. 'You can look.'

I struggled out of the back end of the horse to see Katherine, headless (the horse's head, that is), sitting on a hooded figure in a black robe.

'I'll haunt you,' it muttered. 'I really will.'

'I'll take the chance,' said Katherine, and pulled the hood away. Underneath, red in the face, and more annoyed than we had ever seen him, was Ron.

***

'I started planning it ages ago,' he told us, squirming.

We were sitting in Mr Templeton's office. The man himself was still on stage, which was perhaps fortunate for Ron.

'I even mentioned it to Mr T, in passing like, but he wasn't having it,' he added.

'So he didn't know,' I said.

Ron puffed out his chest. 'Nah. I'm too crafty for him. Look at our takings.'

'Crafty, maybe,' Katherine said, 'but you do realise that you scared half the cast to death.'

'I toned it down!' cried Ron. 'Specially after Ellen nearly had a fit one night, and those mums took their kiddies home. And you can't blame me for that priest showing up, that was nuffink to do with me.'

'That's as may be,' I said. 'But you shouldn't play on people's nerves like that, even if it does bring audiences in. It isn't fair.'

'Couldn't if I wanted to now,' said Ron. 'You've squashed my Aeolian harp. I had the bellows set up lovely an' everything.' He cradled a smashed wooden frame on his lap, its strings all over the place. He shrugged.

'Anyway, you two had best get back on. If there ain't no ghost, the audience'll have to make do with a talking horse.'

'Ah, but there could be a ghost,' said Katherine. 'On stage.'

Ron stared at her. 'I ain't following.'

'I'm hoping we won't regret this,' I said, 'but do you have any spare white sheets?'

A slow grin spread over Ron's face. 'I guess I could lay my hands on one,' he said, 'if you tell me what you've got in mind.'

***

'He's very good, isn't he,' I said to Katherine, from our vantage point deep in the wings.

Katherine giggled quietly. 'Who knew the ghost of Cinderella's mother would be so disruptive?'

As Dobbin, we had introduced Ron in his sheet to Cinderella, and explained that without a physical form, the ghost of Cinderella's mother had tried to catch her attention by all sorts of means. Now that she had pinched a sheet from the castle's linen cupboard, though, things would be much better. And so they were. The ghost hindered Cinderella with the housework, played pranks on the Ugly Sisters, and even found time for a pas de deux with Dobbin while the scene-shifters transformed the stage behind us into a ballroom. The audience's laughter rang in our ears.

'Good work, ladies,' murmured Mr Templeton as he came off stage, grinning from ear to ear. 'We'll have to keep him in the show. I don't suppose you two would consider—'

'It's a very kind offer, Mr Templeton,' I said, 'but one night of stardom is enough. I still have my Christmas shopping to do.'

He sighed. 'Well, join us for the curtain call, anyway.'

The curtain call came all too soon, and Katherine and I reassembled ourselves hastily. 'On you go, horsey,' said someone, giving me a hefty push in the rear, and Dobbin trotted on stage to cheers.

'You'll have to tell me what's happening,' I whispered to Katherine. 'I can't see a thing.'

'The footmen and the servants are on, and the ball guests,' said Katherine. 'Here come Buttons and the Fairy Godmother . . . and the Ugly Sisters.'

The audience cheered louder and louder as the stage filled.

'Cinderella and Prince Charming are here.' I was still gripping Katherine's waist, and felt her frame relax. 'All done.'

But the audience were clapping rhythmically and stamping their feet. Someone shouted words I couldn't make out through the costume. 'What are they saying?' I asked.

The chant grew louder and louder. 'We want the ghost! We want the ghost!'

I twisted round and peeped through my eyeholes, and saw Mr Templeton cup a hand to his ear. 'Can't hear you,' he shouted. 'What did you say?'

'We want the ghost!' the audience chanted happily. Then a massive cheer escalated to a roar. The audience cried, as if with one voice, ‘She’s behind you!’ and burst into a storm of applause.

'This is the first chance I've had to say that you look stunning,' said Connie as we rested from the dancing in a quiet corner of her dining room.

Her party – celebrating not just Christmas but the conclusion of our case and the launch of Fraser's Christmas Bauble sweets – was a great success. The house was warm, the hired string quartet played gentle music as the guests paused for food, and all around us was the buzz of conversation, the swish of ball-dresses and laughter. It felt a hundred times more refined than the Merrymakers, though I wouldn't have been surprised if Cinderella had waltzed in on Prince Charming's arm.

At least if she had, her dress might have made people stop staring at mine. 'You mean I look better than I did as a horse.'

'Don't be silly,' said Connie. 'And stop pulling a face when I'm paying you a compliment. James and Maria were right to persuade you to try that rusty red. You look like the spirit of Autumn. A small one, admittedly.'

'I don't look ridiculous?'

'Honestly, Katherine, you look lovely. Particularly considering the awful get-ups you've worn: flounces, frills, clashing tartan, dots the size of puppies, a horse's head—'

'That was in the course of duty.' But I glanced at our reflections in the big mirror and decided to be more objective. Connie herself was resplendent in a beautiful new dress of light-gold silk embroidered with coloured flowers. My rich, brownish-red damask was unembellished, but the patterns woven into the fabric shimmered. In the soft light of the dining room I saw that despite my fears, the colour really did compliment rather than clash with my hair. 'I'm being ridiculously vain,' I concluded. 'I must have caught it from Margaret.'

'James keeps looking at you with quite a twinkle. Don't wear yourself out with too much dancing.'

'Shh!' I peeped, then hid behind my fan. 'Don't make me blush. I'll look like a lit matchstick.'

'Are you all set for your journey tomorrow? London will be quiet without you.'

'Maybe one day you can come to Berkshire with us for Christmas. It's nice and peaceful in the middle of nowhere.'

'We could stay with the other Lamonts,' said Connie. 'They ask us every year, so we'd be neighbours for a few days. Although Mrs Jones would be so relieved not to have to manage Christmas dinner that she might forget herself and kiss me.'

We both laughed. 'My goodness, what a thought,' I

said. 'Anyway, never mind that now. It's time for presents.' Connie and I were exchanging gifts at the party, as we wouldn't see each other for a few days. 'I hope you like it,' I said, extracting a small package from my bag and passing it over. Knowing each other so well made it somehow harder to choose something unique.

Connie carefully unwrapped the small box – 'Ooh, Liberty's!' – and traced the printed design. She opened it, lifted the charm bracelet from the velvet interior and turned it this way and that. I bit my lip. What if she thought it silly?

She burst out laughing. 'A charm for each of our big cases! A black tulip – a mask – a bonbon! And look, a typewriter charm! You even found a little horse!' She flung her arms around me. 'It's wonderful, thank you so much! And there's room for more charms, too.'

'I'm hoping we'll have more adventures.'

'Of course we shall!'

'Are you sure you like it?'

'Of course I am. It's one of the best presents I've ever had.'

Now Connie was looking pensive, and I felt my face flame. What if I'd misunderstood, and she had meant us to exchange presents at New Year and had nothing to give me?

'Yours was impossible to wrap,' she said.

I blinked. Whatever had she bought? I needed a new desk, but—

Connie looked around, then dropped her voice. 'And you may not like it. But whether you do or not, can you keep it a secret till Christmas Day?'

I glanced at the buffet table. Thirza was trying to restrain Father from putting too many sweet things on his plate. 'Another secret?'

Connie followed my glance. 'Your father sort of helped.'

'He did?'

'Your present is a secret because it's linked with Albert's. You remember I didn't know what to get him? Well, his father once told us that he'd collected information about the Lamonts and the Demerays from when they fled France back in sixteen-whenever-it-was. He showed me a box full of letters and journals and scraps of the families' silk designs.'

'Oh yes!' I exclaimed. 'I'd forgotten. I used to look through it when I was small.'

Connie smiled. 'Of course both your families sold their weaving businesses generations ago, but your uncle Maurice was very proud of his ancestry.'

'Yes, we are too,' I said, puzzled.

'So first I thought of getting Albert a new cravat, woven to copy one of those old designs…'

Perhaps Connie had ordered me a shawl or a scarf. For the life of me I couldn't recall the designs, but they would be lovely. Although a shawl would be easy to wrap – or perhaps it wasn't ready yet?

'Then I found a notebook your uncle Maurice had filled with plans. He wanted to visit the town your families came from, but of course he never did.'

I gave up wondering where this was going, and waited.

'So with your father's help – he was quite giggly, for some reason – I've booked a train and rented a small house in the area, so we can spend a week there in January. It's in the South of France, so hopefully it will be a little warmer than here, and a lot less rainy. We'll leave the children behind, which will be a wrench, but it'll only be ten days, and the grandparents will spoil them rotten.' She beamed at me. 'What do you think?'

'How lovely,' I said. 'Albert will be thrilled.' I meant it, but I felt rather flat.

'Will you?'

'I'm sure you'll have a wonderful time, and you can tell me all about it afterwards. Reg and I can manage the—'

Connie put a hand on my arm. 'Oh no, you've misunderstood! When I said we, I meant the four of us. You, me, Albert and James. Unless you'd rather not come…?' Her smile had vanished, and her blue eyes searched mine.

My mouth dropped open, then I recovered myself. 'It's a brilliant idea!' I said. 'I'd love to come! But what about the agency?'

'I had a word with Reg, and he's more than happy to hold the fort. He mentioned building up his savings; I'm not sure it needs a detective to work out why.'

We both looked across the room. Reg was fussing over Lily, trying to get her to stay in her seat and offering her extra food.

I chuckled. 'I predict a stork in May.'

'Definitely,' said Connie. 'I can't wait to get Albert away from Fraser's.' She blushed.

I grinned at her. 'I just hope James doesn't start writing another novel while we're in France.'

'So you'll come?'

'Of course we shall. It'll be strange without Ed, but you and I have never had a proper holiday together. It'll be wonderful.' I squeezed her hand.

In the other room, the string quartet burst into a lively tune.

'Come on,' I said. 'It's time to dance again. I have no idea how I'll keep all these secrets, I could burst.'

Connie hugged me tight. 'What a Christmas – unexpected cases, mysteries, ghosts and secrets.'

'What do you mean?' I cried. 'It's been the best Christmas ever! Come on, Connie, let's polka!'

Now Read On...

If this is your first encounter with Katherine and Connie, you probably have several unanswered questions. Were they always friends? How did they get involved with a music hall and a former fortune teller? And how did they become detectives?

Fear not, for the full series of six historical mystery novels is at hand! Discover how Katherine and Connie met, and how they got caught up in their first mystery, in *The Case of the Black Tulips*.

The Caster & Fleet Mysteries

The Case of the Black Tulips
The Case of the Runaway Client
The Case of the Deceased Clerk
The Case of the Masquerade Mob
The Case of the Fateful Legacy
The Case of the Crystal Kisses

ACKNOWLEDGEMENTS

Time for the curtain call! First of all, a rousing cheer and many thanks to our beta readers, both for their speed and their feedback: Carol Bissett, Ruth Cunliffe, Christine Downes, Stephen Lenhardt, Val Portelli, and Sim Sansford. And as always, another cheer for our intrepid proofreader, John Croall.

But the final cheer is for you, the reader. We hope you've enjoyed our Christmas mystery, and if you have, some applause in the form of a short review or rating on Amazon or Goodreads would be wonderful. Your feedback helps readers to discover new books (including ours!).

FONT AND IMAGE CREDITS:

Fonts:

Main cover font: Birmingham Titling by Paul Lloyd (freeware): https://www.fontzillion.com/fonts/paul-lloyd/birmingham

Classic font: Libre Baskerville Italic by Impallari Type: https://www.fontsquirrel.com/fonts/libre-baskerville. SIL Open Font License v.1.10: http://scripts.sil.org/OFL

Graphics:

Curtain (rescaled): Spotlight on stage curtain. event and show, fabric and entertainment. vector illustration Free Vector by macrovector at freepik.com: https://www.freepik.com/free-vector/spotlight-stage-curtain-event-show-fabric-entertainment-vector-illustration_11059406.htm.

Cover created using GIMP image editor: www.gimp.org

About Paula Harmon

Paula Harmon was born in North London to parents of English, Scottish and Irish descent. Perhaps feeling the need to add a Welsh connection, her father relocated the family every two years from country town to country town moving slowly westwards until they settled in South Wales when Paula was eight. She later graduated from Chichester University before making her home in Gloucestershire and then Dorset where she has lived since 2005.

She is a civil servant, married with two adult children. Paula has several writing projects underway and wonders where the housework fairies are, because the house is a mess and she can't think why.

https://paulaharmon.com
https://www.facebook.com/pg/paulaharmonwrites
https://twitter.com/Paula_S_Harmon
viewauthor.at/PHAuthorpage

About Liz Hedgecock

Liz Hedgecock grew up in London, England, did an English degree, and then took forever to start writing. After several years working in the National Health Service, some short stories crept into the world. A few even won prizes. Then the stories started to grow longer…

Now Liz travels between the nineteenth and twenty-first centuries, murdering people. To be fair, she does usually clean up after herself.

Liz's reimaginings of Sherlock Holmes, her Pippa Parker cozy mystery series, the Magical Bookshop series, the Caster & Fleet Victorian mystery series (written with Paula Harmon), and the Maisie Frobisher Mysteries are available in ebook and paperback.

Liz lives in Cheshire with her husband and two sons, and when she's not writing or child-wrangling you can usually find her reading, messing about on Twitter, or cooing over stuff in museums and art galleries. That's her story, anyway, and she's sticking to it.

Website/blog: http://lizhedgecock.wordpress.com
Facebook: http://www.facebook.com/lizhedgecockwrites
Twitter: http://twitter.com/lizhedgecock
Goodreads: https://www.goodreads.com/lizhedgecock
Amazon author page: http://author.to/LizH

Books by Paula Harmon

Murder Britannica

AD190 Southern Britain. Lucretia won't let her get-rich-quick scheme be undermined by anything. But a gruesome discovery leads wise-woman Tryssa to start asking awkward questions.

Murder Durnovaria

AD191. All Lucretia wants is her inheritance. But when an old ring appears, her old adversary Tryssa must help local magistrate Amicus discover who would rather kill than reveal long-buried truths.

The Wrong Sort To Die

London 1910. When Dr Margaret Demeray is approached by a stranger called Fox to discover what's killing paupers, she expects justice. What she gets is danger.

The Cluttering Discombobulator

Can everything be fixed with duct tape? Dad thinks so. The story of one man's battle against common sense and the family caught up in the chaos around him.

Kindling

Secrets and mysteries, strangers and friends. Stories as varied and changing as British skies.

The Advent Calendar

Christmas without the hype - stories for midwinter.

The Quest

In a parallel universe, Dorissa and Menilly, descendants of the distrusted dragon people, are desperate to find their runaway brother in a fog-bound city which simmers with unrest and deceit.

The Seaside Dragon

For 7-11 year olds. When Laura and Jane go on holiday to a remote cottage, the worst they expect is no wifi. The last thing they expect is to be battling strange creatures with an ancient grudge.

The Case of the Black Tulips (with Liz Hedgecock)

When Katherine Demeray opens a letter addressed to her missing father, little does she imagine that she will find herself in partnership with socialite Connie Swift, racing against time to solve mysteries and right wrongs. (This is the first of six Caster & Fleet Mysteries)

Weird and Peculiar Tales (with Val Portelli)

Short stories from this world and beyond.

Books by Liz Hedgecock

To check out any of my books, please visit my Amazon author page: http://author.to/LizH. If you follow me there, you'll be notified whenever I release a new book.

Maisie Frobisher Mysteries (3 novels)

When Maisie Frobisher, a bored young Victorian socialite, goes travelling in search of adventure, she finds more than she could ever have dreamt of. Mystery, intrigue and a touch of romance.

Caster & Fleet Mysteries (6 novels, with Paula Harmon)

There's a new detective duo in Victorian London . . . and they're women! Meet Katherine and Connie, two young women who become partners in crime. Solving it, that is!

Pippa Parker Mysteries (6 novels)

Meet Pippa Parker – mum, amateur sleuth, and resident of a quaint English village called Much Gadding. And then the murders began…

The Magical Bookshop (3 short novels)

An eccentric owner, a hostile cat, and a bookshop with a mind of its own. Can Jemma turn around the second-worst secondhand bookshop in London? And can she learn its secrets?

Mrs Hudson & Sherlock Holmes (2 novels)

Mrs Hudson is Sherlock Holmes's elderly landlady. Or is she? Find out her real story here.

Sherlock & Jack (3 novellas)

Jack has been ducking and diving all her life. But when she meets the great detective Sherlock Holmes, they form an unlikely partnership. And Jack discovers that she is more important than she ever realised…

Halloween Sherlock (3 novelettes)

Short dark tales of Sherlock Holmes and Dr Watson, perfect for a grim winter's night.

For children (with Zoe Harmon)

A Christmas Carrot

Printed in Great Britain
by Amazon

56134283R00052